VOLTRON

Battle For the Black Lion

Adapted by Natalie Shaw

WITHDRAWN

Simon Spotlight

New York   London   Toronto   Sydney   New Delhi

SIMON SPOTLIGHT

An imprint of Simon & Schuster Children's Publishing Division
1230 Avenue of the Americas, New York, New York 10020
This Simon Spotlight edition August 2017
DreamWorks Voltron Legendary Defender © 2017 DreamWorks Animation LLC. TM World Events Productions, LLC. All Rights Reserved. All rights reserved, including the right of reproduction in whole or in part in any form. SIMON SPOTLIGHT and colophon are registered trademarks of Simon & Schuster, Inc. For information about special discounts for bulk purchases, please contact Simon & Schuster Special Sales at 1-866-506-1949 or business@simonandschuster.com.
Designed by Nick Sciacca & Brittany Naundorff. The text of this book was set in United Sans Reg.
Manufactured in the United States of America 0617 LAK
2 4 6 8 10 9 7 5 3 1
ISBN 978-1-5344-0923-1 (hc)
ISBN 978-1-5344-0922-4 (pbk)
ISBN 978-1-5344-0924-8 (eBook)

CHAPTER 1

"Thanks to Pidge's modifications, we'll have thirty seconds of cloaking," Shiro said as the Green Lion disappeared into the background of stars.

The five Paladins of Voltron and Princess Allura gathered their courage as they flew from the Castle of Lions to a secret transportation hub of the Galra Empire.

They landed on a craggy moon covered with machinery and snuck on to the base undetected.

When they reached the central control room, the Paladins drew their Bayards. Hunk and Lance's Bayards transformed into energy blasters. Hunk kicked down the door, and with two easy shots, he and Lance took out the robotic henchmen. The rest of the team streamed into the room.

Shiro, the Black Paladin, didn't have a Bayard. He knocked out the Galra lieutenant with his energy hand. Princess Allura restrained the lieutenant with energy cuffs.

Keith covered the door with his Red Bayard, which had transformed into a sword.

The room was clear. Pidge's *katar* transformed back into her Green Bayard. She quickly unpacked the tech she'd made for the mission.

"We only have a few minutes before the next patrol comes by," Shiro told the team. He had been a Galra prisoner and remembered the sentry patrol pattern. "But that should be enough to get what we need," he continued.

Pidge connected her device to the control room computer, then to Shiro's robotic arm. The Galra had transformed his arm while he was their prisoner. It was a constant reminder of

the Galra's cruelty, but it also allowed the team to interface with Galra tech. "I've made some software modifications since the last time we tried to download Galra info," Pidge said.

Now was the moment of truth. The team took a big risk sneaking onto a Galra base. They needed information if they were ever going to stop Emperor Zarkon from conquering the universe.

Pidge's device kicked into action, and the information downloaded at a rapid speed.

"I say we challenge Zarkon to a fight— winner gets the universe," Lance said

playfully, tossing punches into the air. The other Paladins rolled their eyes.

"Zarkon's been building his empire for ten thousand years," Shiro said. "We're not going to tear it down overnight with five inexperienced pilots and one support ship."

The Paladins knew Shiro was right. Since first forming Voltron, they had battled Zarkon's commanders. They had barely survived, even with Princess Allura backing them up from the Castle of Lions.

"We just need some troop locations, then we can start to free planets from the

Galra Empire one by one," Shiro explained. The information finished downloading.

"What does it say?" Keith asked.

Pidge frowned, and said, "Nothing useful. Just a schedule of the ships coming in and out." The mission had been a bust. It was time to head back to the castle.

Suddenly Princess Allura's eyes widened. "Hold on, Pidge! Do you know where that ship is headed?" she asked, pointing outside.

"It's scheduled to be here for a half hour and then head off to Galra Central Command," Pidge replied.

"*That's* where they have the information we need," Princess Allura exclaimed. "And I'm going to sneak aboard that ship and get it!"

That's when Princess Allura's adviser, Coran, chimed in over the communication device. "Oh, I'd rather you didn't, Princess," he said from the Castle of Lions. It was in Castleship mode and hidden behind a planet nearby. As one of two surviving Alteans, he

knew only a member of the Altean royal family could pilot the Castleship through wormholes. Sneaking onto the Galra base with the team was one thing. Boarding an enemy ship bound for Central Command was another. If anything happened to Princess Allura, the Castle of Lions would be a sitting duck and the team would have no escape.

"I'm a part of this fight against Zarkon as much as anyone," Princess Allura said, remembering how Zarkon destroyed her home planet. "I'm going."

"How are you going to get in?" Keith asked.

"I'm going to walk right through the front entrance," Princess Allura announced. She closed her eyes, concentrated her energy, and suddenly, her skin turned purple. She grew taller, and she looked Galra!

"How the heck did you do that?" asked Hunk.

"The Alteans have the ability to blend in with local people. It has made us

great explorers and diplomats throughout our history," she replied calmly. To complete the transformation, she borrowed armor from the lieutenant they had restrained with energy cuffs.

"Shiro's robotic arm is made of Galra tech," Pidge said. "You'll need him to interface with Galra systems."

With only a half hour to complete their mission, Princess Allura and Shiro set out to collect the information and return to the Green Lion.

CHAPTER 2

On the loading deck of the Galra transportation base, Princess Allura waited to board the Galra ship. She had stolen a crate, and Shiro was hiding inside.

"Halt," a Galra lieutenant said to Princess Allura. She watched as a hooded figure and two Galra workers unloaded containers of glowing yellow liquid from the ship. Once they were passed, the lieutenant allowed Princess Allura to board.

Keith was watching from the control room of the transportation base. "What do you think they have in all those giant containers?" he asked.

"Sporks," Hunk joked without skipping a beat. "The Galra have advanced technology. Surely they've learned that it's foolish to have forks and spoons when one tool will do the job."

"I'm gonna check it out," Keith said.

"How about you just lay low and don't blow our cover?" Lance suggested.

Before Lance could stop him, Keith ran out.

After ditching the crate, Shiro and Princess Allura snuck into the Galra ship's computer room. Shiro quickly knocked out the two sentries at the desk.

"Watch the door," Shiro said, tossing Princess Allura a Galra energy blaster.

"Got it," Princess Allura said.

Shiro placed his robotic hand onto the computer scanner and told Pidge over his

comm to start downloading information.

"We're in!" Pidge said, connecting the link. Finally, they would have information to use to fight Zarkon!

Meanwhile, Keith followed the hooded figure he had seen on the loading deck. The figure was a Druid, a member of a powerful clan of magic wielders serving Zarkon. The Druid entered the transportation base and then went into a room lined with shelves of glowing yellow liquid.

Out of sight, Keith watched as the Druid shot dark magic into a container, turning the contents purple.

Keith sent a video to his teammates. "You gotta see this," he whispered into his headset.

"I've never seen anything like that," Coran admitted from the bridge of the Castleship.

"What *is* that?" Pidge asked from the transportation base control room. She and Hunk had been tinkering with a sentry's circuits to get it to help them. Pidge, Hunk, and

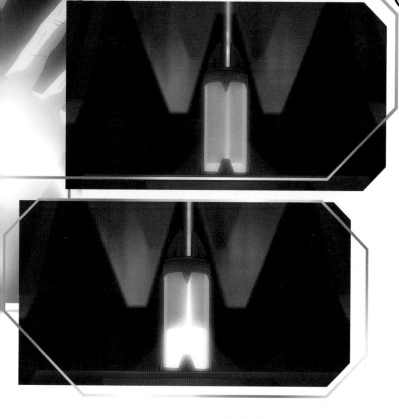

Lance all looked on in disbelief as the robot suddenly spoke.

"The material is Quintessence, the substance that powers the entire Galra Empire," it said. "The equipment on this base is used for refining raw Quintessence material that is brought here from throughout the galaxy."

"They've found a way to manufacture pure

energy!" Coran said into his comm.

"I'm going to steal some of this Quint-whatever," Keith whispered back.

Keith dove quickly over a conveyer belt and grabbed a small vial of Quintessence, but the Druid sensed his presence.

In a flash, the Druid teleported in front of Keith and blasted him with dark magic. Keith flew backward across the room. The dark magic burned through his armor. Suddenly, Keith felt searing pain in his arm. He dropped the vial of Quintessence.

"I need help now!" Keith gasped into his comm. He drew his Bayard as the Druid prepared another attack.

Back on the Galra ship, Shiro continued
to extract information until the computer
recognized Shiro's robotic arm. Suddenly it
flashed an alarm. "Fugitive prisoner detected.
Remain where you are. Security alerted," a
voice said over the ship's comm.

"We have to go!" Allura exclaimed. Shiro
removed his arm from the computer. He and

Princess Allura ran back toward their team and the Green Lion. Sentries ran down the hall after them, firing their energy blasters.

"Pidge, fire up the Green Lion," Shiro said over his comm. "We're coming in hot!"

Still in horrible pain, Keith steadied himself against a container of Quintessence.

The Druid was about to strike Keith again when the room suddenly shook. The Green Lion blasted a hole in the ceiling. Debris rained down, and the Druid stumbled, accidentally sending his dark magic into the container. It shattered and covered Keith with Quintessence.

The Green Lion landed beside Keith, and the Druid teleported away.

"Get in!" Pidge said from inside the lion. "We gotta get Shiro and Princess Allura."

As Keith boarded the lion, he noticed something strange: the Quintessence had somehow healed the burns on his arm!

CHAPTER 3

Aboard the Galra ship, Princess Allura and Shiro ran into an escape-pod hangar.

"All personnel prepare for emergency takeoff," the voice on the ship's comm said.

"Hurry! We can't leave once the ship goes into hyperspeed!" Princess Allura said. With no time to lose, she activated the escape-pod launch. The hangar doors began to close.

Suddenly, the sentries were at the doors They wedged their hands between the doors

and stopped them from interlocking. Princess Allura dropped her blaster and held the doors closed with her incredible Altean strength.

"The pod is taking off. Get in!" Princess Allura ordered Shiro.

Shiro stood firm. "I'm not leaving you!"

"You have to!" she said. She let go of the doors and threw Shiro into the escape pod. It sealed shut. Sentries streamed into the hangar and captured Princess Allura.

Shiro looked on powerlessly. The escape pod launched. Shiro watched from space as the Galra ship went into hyperspeed. In an instant, the ship and Princess Allura were gone.

Shiro and the rest of the team reunited aboard the Castle of Lions.

"Where's Princess Allura?" Keith asked Shiro.

"She sacrificed herself to save me," Shiro said sadly.

"So she's still on that ship?" Pidge asked.

"The ship that's headed to Zarkon's Central Command?" Hunk added.

"The place that's way too dangerous for us to attack?" Keith finished.

Shiro nodded. "It doesn't matter how dangerous it is. We can't let Zarkon get Princess Allura."

Princess Allura was delivered directly to Zarkon's Central Command. In her Galra disguise, she was presented to Zarkon as his prisoner. His most trusted adviser, Haggar, stood at his side.

"Princess Allura," Zarkon said.

Surprised that Zarkon knew her real identity, Princess Allura let her Galra disguise fall away. "You monster! You destroyed Altea!" she yelled. "Voltron is going to put an end to your empire."

Zarkon was calm.

"No, it will only make me more powerful. Your father, King Alfor, knew that as well as I. That's why he led me to believe he destroyed Voltron all those years ago. Now, your Paladins will come for you and deliver Voltron to me, and with it, the key to unimaginable power."

Zarkon gathered his top commanders and told them to allow Voltron inside the border of Central Command.

"Once in, Voltron won't get out," Haggar promised.

Back on the Castleship, the Paladins planned their rescue mission.

Using the information Shiro had down-loaded from the Galra ship, Pidge quickly found Zarkon's Central Command. It was enormous.

"If there was just a way to get us *close* to Central Command unseen . . . ," Shiro lamented.

"I think we have enough of Princess Allura's energy stored in the Castleship to make one wormhole jump," Coran said. "But without Princess Allura, we won't have enough energy to wormhole back out."

"We're *not* leaving without her," Shiro said. "We'll grab the princess and be on our way before they know what hit them."

The team agreed. The Castleship quickly jumped through a wormhole and arrived at Central Command.

Everyone rushed to their lions. They soared into space in formation and became one unit as they formed Voltron the Legendary Defender.

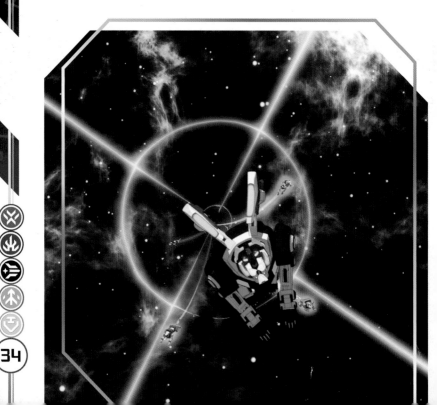

Zarkon and his commanders watched as Voltron approached. "Engage the particle barrier!" Zarkon barked. "Attack!"

In an instant, the barrier formed around Central Command and Voltron. Zarkon had Voltron trapped.

Then a Galra fighter ship launched from Central Command came in for an attack.

"Form sword!" Shiro commanded. With the sword, Voltron sliced the fighter ship in half.

"More trouble, straight ahead!" Lance warned.

As more ships flew toward Voltron, Shiro said, "Form shoulder cannon!"

The cannon's lasers took out dozens of fighters and cleared a path to Central Command.

"We're coming, Allura!" Shiro yelled as they flew.

Voltron held up the sword and was about to cut into Central Command . . . when suddenly the sword vanished.

"We lost the sword!" Keith shouted. "Something's malfunctioning!"

Sure enough, on the Black Lion, an alarm sounded. Shiro's system was jammed. He tried everything, but the Black Lion was paralyzed.

"Somebody do something!" Lance said. "Voltron's frozen up!"

"I can't hold it!" Shiro said, trying to regain control of his lion.

Voltron was forced apart, but that was the least of the Paladins' problems. An entire fleet of Galra ships was headed their way. Without Voltron, the Paladins didn't stand a chance against their enemy.

CHAPTER 4

The five lions of Voltron were surrounded by Galra fighter ships. Escape was hopeless.

"Coran attack!" Coran said, firing the Castleship's laser beam. He took out the ships attacking the lions. "I've waited ten thousand years for this!" he said. With Coran covering them, the Paladins flew into action, all except for Shiro.

Inside the Black Lion, Shiro struggled to communicate with his lion. Someone or something was interfering. Then he heard Zarkon's voice all around him. "You can't fight it. Your connection is weak," he said. Shiro's monitors turned purple, and he was ejected from the Black Lion!

Shiro crashed into the hull of Central Command. His jet pack was damaged. He looked back and saw a tractor beam pulling the Black Lion toward Central Command.

How did I get ejected? Who was controlling the ship? Shiro wondered.

"I'm going for the Black Lion," Shiro told the Paladins. "You guys get the princess!"

Shiro used his energy hand to cut a hole into the side of the ship. He climbed in.

Haggar was waiting for him. "So, the champion returns . . . ," she said mysteriously.

Shiro lunged at the witch, but she vanished. Then she used dark magic to make hundreds of Haggars appeared around him!

"I made you strong," the real Haggar yelled, revealing that she had given Shiro his robotic arm. "And *this* is how you repay me?" She struck him with dark energy, and he fell back with a wound on his side. He screamed in pain.

Meanwhile, Pidge, Lance, and Hunk scanned for Princess Allura's location.

"This is it! The princess is in this part of the ship!" Hunk said.

"How do we get in?" Lance asked.

"Maybe I can try hacking one of their cargo bays," Pidge suggested

"I have a better idea," Hunk said, and rammed the head of the Yellow Lion through the hull of Central Command.

"Looks like we've got to cover Hunk's butt,"

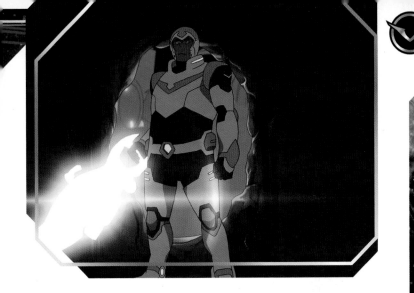

Lance said to Pidge, only half joking. Galra fighter ships swarmed the Yellow Lion.

Inside Central Command, Hunk ran out of the lion's mouth. With a few shots from his energy cannon, he blasted a hole in Princess Allura's cell.

"What are you doing here?" Princess Allura asked. "Tell me you didn't bring Voltron to Zarkon's Central Command! Where's the Black Lion?"

As if on cue, they heard Shiro screaming through their headsets.

"We have to save Shiro!" Princess Allura said.

Outside, the Black Lion was still being drawn into Central Command. Without all five lions, the Paladins wouldn't be able to form Voltron. Keith flew at top speed and knocked the Black Lion off course!

That was when Zarkon came outside to the hull of the ship. He had the Black Bayard! It had been missing since the fall of Altea, but Coran recognized it immediately.

"Keith, get out of there. Now! He's too powerful!" Coran yelled over the comm.

Instead, Keith listened to his instincts and attacked. "This is my chance to put an end to the Galra Empire. I have to take it!"

Inside
Central Command,
Princess Allura and
Hunk dicovered Shiro
surrounded by Druids.

It was Haggar's illusion.

"Which one is the real one?" Hunk asked Princess Allura.

"And now, your time is over!" Haggar warned Shiro.

Princess Allura pointed. "There!" she yelled. Hunk blasted his energy cannon at the real Haggar.

As Haggar turned to block the blast, Shiro swiped at her with his energy hand. Haggar was outnumbered and teleported away.

"Where's the scary lady?" Hunk asked.

"We have to go now!" Allura yelled. She pulled Hunk along with her and Shiro. Now it was time to save the Black Lion.

CHAPTER 5

On the hull of Central Command, Keith fired the Red Lion's mouth cannon at Zarkon. He blocked the blast by using the Black Bayard as a giant shield.

"You may have a lion, but its power is weak in your hands," Zarkon said. "You cannot stop me. The Black Lion will finally be returned to its original Paladin!"

Zarkon was the original Black Paladin! Keith didn't have time to think about that. Zarkon

turned the Black Bayard from a shield into an energy cannon and then blasted the Red Lion.

Keith recovered and engaged the Red Lion's mouth blade. Zarkon transformed the Black Bayard back into a sword and got ready for the attack.

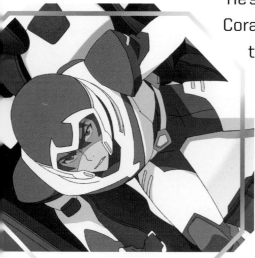

"He's too powerful!" Coran told Keith over the comm.

Keith ignored the warning. Instead, he charged at Zarkon again.

Zarkon's sword split in two, becoming an energy chain that whipped at the Red Lion's leg and made it crash into the hull of Central Command. The Red Lion's screens started to flicker, but Keith could still make out Zarkon sprinting toward him with his sword drawn.

"No!" Keith yelled.

He jammed the controls forward, and the inside of the lion began to glow. It responded to his extreme emotion by revealing a hidden

power! A back rail gun appeared on the lion's back and shot a laser beam at Zarkon.

Zarkon split the beam with his sword and struck the Red Lion.

"You fight like a Galra soldier," Zarkon said to Keith, "but not for long." He prepared to deliver a final blow with his sword.

"No! No! No!" Keith fumbled at the controls, trying to get the battered lion to respond.

Bam! The Black Lion blasted Zarkon with its mouth cannon and sent him flying. Then the Black Lion swooped in to save Keith and the Red Lion.

"I got you, buddy!" Shiro said from the Black Lion. He was just in time.

CHAPTER 6

All five lions returned to the Castleship. Princess Allura took the controls. She tried to form a wormhole. There was just one problem: the Galra particle barrier was blocking Allura's energy.

"What's going on?" Hunk said, panicked.

"They have us surrounded!" Coran yelled.

Inside Central Command, a commander ordered the Galran fleet to corner the Castleship.

"Send in everything we've got!" the commander ordered.

He had no idea that another Galra commander had just snuck into Central Command's engine room. With a masterful flick of the wrist, he flung an ancient blade into the back of the sentry.

The rogue commander pulled a switch.

Instantly, the particle barrier vanished!

Outside, on the Castleship, everyone was shocked to see a wormhole appear!

"What just happened?" Pidge asked.

"Who cares?" Hunk said. "Wormhole!"

Zarkon fumed as the Castleship escaped through the wormhole and out of his reach. Haggar too was enraged. She summoned a huge bolt of dark magic and shot it at the wormhole just before it closed. The Castleship began to spin out of control!

"The integrity of the wormhole has been compromised! It's breaking down!" Coran shouted.

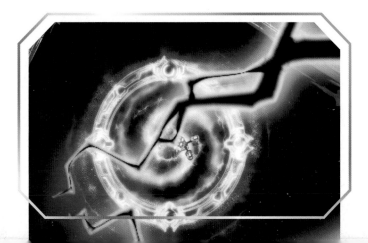

"What does that mean?" Lance yelled back.

"It means we have no control over where we're headed!" Coran said.

As the Castleship and the five lions were separated, they went into a free fall.

They had won the battle for the Black Lion, but now they were scattered across the universe with the knowledge that Zarkon was even more powerful than they had imagined!